Magic Puppy

A New Beginning

SUE BENTLEY

Illustrated by Angela Swan

GROSSET & DUNLAP
Published by the Penguin Group
Penguin Group (USA) Inc., 375 Hudson Street, New York, New York 10014, USA
Penguin Group (Canada), 90 Eglinton Avenue East, Suite 700,
Toronto, Ontario M4P 2Y3, Canada
(a division of Pearson Penguin Canada Inc.)
Penguin Books Ltd., 80 Strand, London WC2R 0RL, England
Penguin Group Ireland, 25 St. Stephen's Green, Dublin 2, Ireland
(a division of Penguin Books Ltd.)
Penguin Group (Australia), 250 Camberwell Road, Camberwell, Victoria 3124, Australia
(a division of Pearson Australia Group Pty. Ltd.)
Penguin Books India Pvt. Ltd., 11 Community Centre, Panchsheel Park,
New Delhi—110 017, India
Penguin Group (NZ), 67 Apollo Drive, Rosedale, North Shore 0632, New Zealand
(a division of Pearson New Zealand Ltd.)
Penguin Books (South Africa) (Pty.) Ltd., 24 Sturdee Avenue,
Rosebank, Johannesburg 2196, South Africa

Penguin Books Ltd., Registered Offices:
80 Strand, London WC2R 0RL, England

Text copyright © 2008 Sue Bentley. Illustrations copyright © 2008 Angela Swan. Cover
illustration copyright © 2008 Andrew Farley. First printed in Great Britain in 2008 by
Penguin Books Ltd. First published in the United States in 2009 by Grosset & Dunlap, a
division of Penguin Young Readers Group, 345 Hudson Street, New York, New York 10014.
GROSSET & DUNLAP is a trademark of Penguin Group (USA) Inc. Printed in the U.S.A.

Library of Congress Cataloging-in-Publication Data is available.

ISBN 978-0-448-45044-5

40 39 38 37 36 35 34 33 32

To Cindy—first and best-beloved,
who was happy in a doll's pram.

Prologue

Storm whimpered as he crawled into the cave. Behind the young silver-gray wolf, stars glimmered in the purple sky.

Suddenly, a piercing howl echoed in the night air.

"Shadow!" Storm gasped, trembling with fear.

The fierce lone wolf who had attacked Storm and the Moon-claw pack was close by. Storm knew he had to disguise himself, and quickly!

There was a dazzling gold flash and a fountain of golden sparks that lit up the back of the cave for a brief second.

Where the wolf cub had just stood, there now crouched a tiny, sandy golden retriever puppy with floppy ears and twinkling midnight-blue eyes.

Storm's little puppy heart beat fast. In that split second of light, he had seen his mother, the she-wolf, lying crumpled against a rock.

"Mother?" he whined, plunging deeper into the cave.

"Storm?" Canista lifted her head to answer him in a velvety growl.

In the dim light Storm could see his mother's heaving sides and hear her rapid breathing. He felt a new surge of panic. "You are hurt! Did Shadow attack you, too?"

Canista nodded weakly. "His bite is poisoned. It drains my strength."

Storm's blue eyes flared with sorrow and anger. "Shadow has already killed my father and my three litter brothers. I will face Shadow and fight him!"

"Bravely said, my son. But now is not the time. You are the only cub left of our Moon-claw pack. Go to the other world. Use this puppy disguise to hide. Return when your magic is stronger. Then, together, we will fight Shadow." Canista's head flopped back tiredly as she finished speaking.

Storm bowed his head. He did not want to leave her, but he knew his mother was right.

The sound of mighty paws and a thunderous snarl echoed from the mouth of the cave.

"Go, Storm. Save yourself," Canista growled urgently.

Storm's sandy fur ignited with gold

sparks. He whined softly as he felt the power building inside him. The golden light around him grew brighter. And brighter . . .

Chapter
★ONE★

Lily Benson felt a leap of excitement as her dad pulled up outside Greengates riding stables.

"Yay! I love Saturday afternoons. I get to spend hours and hours with ponies!" she cried, jumping out of the car.

Lily went around to the open window and bent down to kiss her dad's cheek.

Mr. Benson laughed. "Careful you don't get pony-overload!"

"There's no such thing," Lily said. Her bedroom walls were covered with posters of ponies and her bookcase was crammed with riding books and magazines.

"What a shame. I was hoping you might stop bugging your mom and me to buy you one!" her dad said.

He was only joking, but Lily felt a pang. She was desperate for a pony of her own. But her parents were worried about the hard work and amount of time it would take to care for it. Lily knew they were hoping she'd be satisfied with having free rides in exchange for helping out at Greengates.

"I'll never stop asking in a zillion years. Ponies rule, Dad!" she said.

"You've got a one-track mind, Lily Benson. Have a good time. See you later," he called, steering away from the curb.

Lily sighed. She waved good-bye and then went into the stable yard.

The main stable buildings were built around two sides of a square. A large gate at one end led to the grazing field. Just beyond the field Lily could see the house where Janie Green who ran Greengates lived.

Janie was outside the tack room with Treacle and Taffy, two of the smaller ponies. Two young children in riding gear stood waiting, ready to mount.

Janie looked up and smiled warmly as Lily approached. She had a round pretty face with twinkling brown eyes and was always cheerful. "Hi, Lily. I hope you're feeling energetic. We're fully booked this afternoon."

"Hi, Janie," Lily said. She patted Taffy's neck and stroked Treacle's nose. "What do you want me to do first?"

"You could give Don a hand with the cleaning, if you don't mind. He's over at Bandit's stall," Janie said.

"Okay," Lily said happily. Bandit was her favorite pony. She was a sweet-natured palomino with a golden-tan coat and a pale mane and tail. Lily would have loved to own a pony just like her.

As Lily went off to find the stable boy she saw even more young riders arriving with their parents. It looked like it was going to be a hectic afternoon.

Lily said hello to Bandit for a few minutes, before spending the next hour or so forking up droppings, wheeling them over to the pile, and spreading fresh bedding.

Riders and ponies came and went. Lily

A New Beginning

lent a hand where it was needed. It was
a hot day and she was soon red-faced
and sweaty.

"Why don't you take a break and go
and get a drink?" Don suggested as she
helped him fill the hay nets and water
buckets. He was tall and wiry, with dark-
red hair, freckles, and a thin face.

"Phew! I think I will," Lily said, pushing a strand of damp blond hair back from her forehead.

She went to the stable's kitchen and had a long, cold drink of orange juice.

As Lily was walking back past the grazing fields, she noticed some trash blowing around on the grass and went to pick it up.

"Thanks, Lily. You're doing a great job!" Janie Green called, pausing to rest the heavy saddle she was carrying on the fence.

"It makes me so mad when people leave stuff behind. Don't they care that a plastic bag could kill a pony if it eats it?" Lily said indignantly.

"I don't think they give it a thought. Maybe they'd be more careful if they did—but not everyone's into horses."

Lily shrugged. "That's their loss, then!"

"I'm with you on that!" Janie said, smiling. "Have you persuaded your parents to buy you a pony yet?"

Lily made a face, thinking miserably of the earlier conversation with her dad.

"I take it that's a sore point," Janie said.

Lily nodded. "I still have to convince them that I can fit taking care of a pony around my schoolwork. Mom and Dad think it would be too much for me and I should wait until I'm older."

"They might be right, you know," Janie said gently. "Looking after a pony is a big commitment and there are no days off."

Lily felt her spirits sink. She thought Janie would be on her side!

"Do you want to take Bandit out? We just got a cancellation, so she's free for a couple of hours," Janie said.

Lily brightened immediately at the thought of a longer free ride than usual. "Really? I can take her out by myself?" she asked delightedly.

Janie nodded. "You've ridden her plenty of times and she's used to you. You can take her along the bridle paths, but don't go beyond the woods. Okay?"

Lily nodded, feeling proud that Janie trusted her. "Thanks, Janie! That's awesome!"

She dashed straight across to Bandit, who was already tacked up. "Hello, girl. We're going for a ride," she crooned, stroking the pony's nose.

Bandit gave a friendly neigh and nuzzled Lily's palm. Lily buckled on her riding hat before mounting the palomino pony and using her heels to nudge her forward.

They trotted out of Greengates and turned onto the bridle path that ran down the edge of a field. The path branched farther on and Lily took the way to the woods.

Other riders from the stables passed her on their way back.

As she and Bandit entered the shade of the trees, Lily's mind drifted into a wonderful daydream. It was easy to imagine that Bandit was her own pony and they were alone. The sound of other riders was muffled and she was screened from them by the thick

bushes. Sunlight filtered through the leaves and speckled everything with spots of light.

"I wish you were mine," Lily said dreamily, leaning forward to pat Bandit's satiny neck.

Suddenly Bandit stumbled on a tree root and the reins were jerked right out of Lily's hands.

"Oh!" Lily pitched forward and fell right over the pony's neck. As the ground rushed up to meet her she closed her eyes, ready for the painful landing.

Chapter
★ TWO ★

The collision with the ground never came.

With a dazzling golden flash and a crackle of sparks, Lily found herself jerking to a sudden halt. Her eyes flew open in shock and she saw that she was caught inside a huge glowing golden net, in midair, half a foot above the ground!

Very slowly, Lily felt herself float down and land gently on some leaves. With a fizzing noise, the glowing net broke up into golden sparks and then melted away into the leaves.

Lily sat up, blinking confusedly.

Her first thought was for Bandit. She whipped around and was relieved to see the pony nibbling some grass in a small clearing a few feet away.

"Your riding creature is fine. I hope that you are not injured," said a strange voice.

Lily stiffened. "W–who said that?"

A tiny puppy with sandy fur, floppy ears, and huge midnight–blue eyes crawled out from beneath a pile of leaves. "I did. My name is Storm of the Moon–claw pack. What are you? And what is the name of your pack?" it woofed.

Lily's jaw dropped as she stared at the puppy in utter amazement. She felt like

pinching herself to make sure she wasn't dreaming. But she saw that the puppy was looking at her quizzically as if waiting for her to respond.

"I'm a g-girl. A human . . . I'm L-Lily. Lily Benson," she found herself stammering. "But I don't know what you mean about a pack."

"A human? I have heard of these." Storm's silky forehead wrinkled in a frown. Lily saw that he was beginning to tremble. "Can I trust you, Lily? I come from far away and I need your help."

Lily was still having difficulty taking this in, but she didn't want to frighten this amazing puppy away. He was absolutely gorgeous with the brightest midnight-blue eyes she had ever seen and big soft paws that looked too big for his body.

Very slowly she got up onto her knees and reached out her hand.

To Lily's delight, Storm edged closer and brushed her fingers with his damp little nose. His tail wagged nervously. Despite being so scared, the tiny puppy seemed to trust her.

"Why do you need my help?" she asked gently.

Storm's deep-blue eyes flashed with anger and sadness. "A lone wolf called Shadow attacked us. My father and brothers were killed and my mother is sick and in hiding. Shadow wants to lead the Moon-claw wolf pack, but the others will not follow him as long as I am alive."

"*Wolf* pack? But you're a pup—" Lily stopped as Storm held up a velvety sandy paw and began backing away.

There was another dazzling bright flash and a burst of gold sparks showered over Lily, crackling around her feet on the ground.

"Oh!" Lily rubbed her eyes, blinded for a second. When she could see again, she saw that the tiny sandy puppy was gone. In its place now stood a majestic

young wolf with thick silver-gray fur
and glowing midnight-blue eyes.

"Storm?" Lily gasped, eyeing the
wolf's large teeth and thick neck-ruff
that glimmered with hundreds of gold
sparks like tiny yellow diamonds.

"Yes, Lily, it is me," Storm said in a
deep velvety growl.

Before Lily could get used to seeing
Storm as his magnificent real self, there

21

was a final gold flash and he appeared once again as a cute sandy puppy.

"Wow! You really are a wolf. That's an awesome disguise," she said, getting up from her knees.

Storm began trembling again. "Not if Shadow's magic finds me. Will you help me hide?"

Lily's heart went out to the helpless puppy. "Of course I will. You can live with . . ." She trailed off as she remembered her parents' rules about having no house pets. They'd probably insist on taking Storm to the pet care center. There must be some way she could help the tiny puppy. "Maybe I could smuggle you into my house, but I don't see how I can hide you for long," she said thoughtfully.

"Do not worry. I will use my magic so that only you will be able to see and hear me," Storm woofed.

"You can make yourself invisible? Wow!" Lily breathed. "No problem, then. You're coming home with me. Just let me catch Bandit. By the time we get back to Greengates, it'll be time for Dad to pick me up."

A few minutes later, as she cradled Storm in her lap on Bandit's back, a big

smile spread across Lily's face. Never in her wildest dreams had she imagined having a magic puppy for a friend!

Chapter
★ THREE ★

"You should sleep in here in case Mom or Dad gets suspicious," Lily told Storm, spreading an old coat in the bottom of her closet. "But when no one's around, you can get on my bed."

Storm looked in the closet and then padded around her bedroom, sniffing everything and exploring. "This is a good place."

"Glad you like it!" Lily said, beaming at him. "Are you hungry?"

The tiny puppy barked eagerly.

"Okay. I'll go and raid the kitchen to

see what I can find. I won't be long."

Lily dashed downstairs. Luckily her dad was in the garden cutting the lawn and her mom had just gone out to her yoga class. She found some leftover chicken in the fridge and quickly broke a piece off for Storm.

Back upstairs, she watched as Storm ate hungrily and then sat back licking his lips. "That was delicious. I like human food."

"I'll get you some dog food later," Lily said.

Storm nodded. "Good. We will go hunting together!"

"I couldn't do that!" Lily said, horrified. "Anyway, there's no need. The store at the end of the street sells dog food in cans. I'll buy some with my

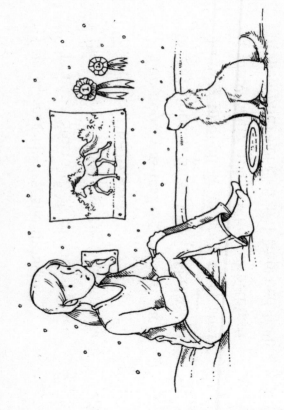

allowance," she told him.

Storm yawned, showing his sharp

little teeth. "I think that I will rest now."

Padding over to the closet, he curled up

on the old coat with a contented sigh

and promptly went to sleep.

Lily watched the tiny puppy's furry

sides rising and falling. Almost

immediately his paws twitched as he

started dreaming. *He must be exhausted*

from his long journey, she thought.

Leaving Storm to sleep, Lily reached for a book of pony stories and stretched out on her bed to read.

The book was really good and she hardly noticed time passing. She was halfway through an exciting story about a pony being stolen, when something leaped onto her bed and launched itself on top of her.

Lily almost jumped out of her skin. "Storm! You scared me!" she said, laughing as she rolled over onto her back. "Did you have a good nap?"

"Yes, thank you. I feel safe here with you," Storm woofed happily. Plonking his big soft paws on her book, he leaned up and began licking her chin.

Lily wrapped her arms around his

plump little sandy body and gave him a cuddle. After a couple of minutes, Storm squirmed free and sprang onto the rug with a surprisingly loud thud for a tiny puppy.

"I would like to go outside now!"

"Okay," Lily said, getting up off the bed. "Our garden's not very big, but there's a field nearby. I'll take you for a walk over there."

Storm gave an eager little bark and followed her downstairs.

As they reached the hall, her dad appeared at the living room door. He had a frown on his face. "What was all that thumping upstairs? It sounded like a herd of elephants."

"Dad! I . . . er . . . thought you were outside," Lily gasped in panic.

She quickly shifted around, trying to stand in front of Storm before she suddenly remembered that he was invisible. Then, realizing how strange that must look, she began bending and stretching her arms. "Whew! Whew!" she puffed for added emphasis. "Just doing some exercise. I'm trying to get in shape. I was about to come and tell you that I'm going out for a jog around the field!"

Her dad raised his eyebrows as Lily did a jumping jack. "Well, I guess that's a good idea. Maybe I'll come with you. I could use some exercise, too."

"No!" Lily said hastily. "Someone . . . um . . . from school might see me. I'll look like a real baby if I'm trailing around after you."

"Excuse me for trying to cramp your

31

style," her dad joked. "What's brought this new fitness fad on?"

"I want to be ready for when I get my own pony! It's going to be hard work looking after it," Lily replied.

Her dad rolled his eyes. "I should have known what was at the bottom of this! Do you ever think of anything else beside ponies?"

"Nope! Well, actually, yes! But you wouldn't believe me if I told you!" Lily said, glancing at Storm who was waiting by the front door. She jogged toward him before her dad could ask anymore awkward questions. "See you later!"

Chapter
★ FOUR ★

As Lily put her school books into her bag on Monday morning, Storm sat watching her.

She smiled at him. "I love having you living here with me, but I have to go out for a few hours. Try not to get bored and chew my rug or anything, or Mom will freak!"

"I will not do anything like that," Storm yapped indignantly.

"Sorry. Sometimes I forget you're not an ordinary puppy," Lily said, bending down to pet his silky ears. "It's a shame

there was only time for a quick walk around the field before breakfast. I'll take you out for a really long walk when I get back from school. Promise."

Storm looked up at her curiously. "What is school?"

"It's a place where kids go to learn. Teachers tell us stuff and give us homework to do and we do projects and all kinds of things," Lily explained.

"School sounds interesting. I will come with you," Storm decided.

Lily grinned. "I wish you could, but pets aren't allowed . . ." She paused as she had a second thought. "Hey! Maybe you *can* come if you stay invisible! But you'd have to be really quiet and stay close to me. Mr. Poke, our class teacher, is very strict."

Storm's face brightened and his little sandy tail started wagging with excitement. "I will make sure that no one will know I'm there—except you, Lily!"

"Cool! Let's go!" Lily put her back-pack on the floor and opened it up. "It might be best if you got inside. I have to cross some busy roads."

Storm jumped into her bag and settled next to her books and gym clothes. Lily put on her bag, said good-bye to her parents, and headed out of the front door.

"We'll probably meet Freema and Katy, my friends from class, on the way. I can't wait to see their faces when I tell them about you!" she said to Storm.

There was a scuffling noise from her bag. Storm popped his head out, his big dewy eyes looking into Lily's. "You cannot tell anyone my secret. Promise me, Lily," he woofed seriously.

Lily was disappointed. She had always wanted a pet to tell her friends about, especially a pony, but she had been really excited at the thought that she might be able to share her amazing magic puppy friend. She'd do anything if it would help keep Storm safe, though. "Okay, I promise. Cross my heart and hope to die," she said.

Storm nodded, satisfied.

As Lily and Storm reached the school gate, they saw Freema and Katy. There was another girl with them whom Lily hadn't seen before.

"Hi, Katy. Hi, Freema," Lily greeted her friends.

"Hi, Lily. This is my cousin, Adjoa," Freema explained. "She just moved here and is going to be in our class."

Adjoa was tall with shiny black hair, an oval face, and big brown eyes, just like Freema.

Lily smiled at her. "Welcome to our school, Adjoa."

"Thanks," Adjoa said shyly.

"Did you help out at Greengates this weekend?" Katy asked Lily as they walked into the school grounds.

Lily nodded. "It was great. I had an extra-long ride on Bandit. Janie let me take her up to the woods by myself."

"Cool!" Katy said.

"Do you like riding?" Adjoa asked Lily.

"It's my favorite thing in the whole world!" Lily replied. "How about you?"

"Adjoa loves ponies, too!" Freema said. She nudged her cousin. "Tell Lily about your pony."

Lily's eyes widened. "You've got your own pony? You're so lucky! What's its name?"

"Pixie. She's gorgeous and I love her to pieces," Adjoa said. "You can come over one night after school and meet her if you like."

"Thanks. I'd love to," Lily said, beaming.

In the classroom, Lily took her usual seat next to Katy. She put her bag on the floor, so that Storm could jump out.

Storm gave himself a shake and then trotted off to sniff around the room.

Mr. Poke took attendance. "And just before we begin," he said, looking up, "I'd like to welcome Adjoa Hardiker to the class."

Adjoa smiled shyly as everyone clapped, including Lily.

A few minutes later, Lily was leaning over to watch Storm. She smiled to herself as the tiny puppy weaved in and out of the desks, his sandy tail wagging.

A voice called out, but Lily was engrossed by Storm's cute antics.

"Lily Benson, can you stop daydreaming and take out your history book, please?" the teacher's sarcastic voice said. Mr. Poke had a bald head with a fuzzy rim of hair around his ears. He had a way of looking down his nose when he was annoyed.

Lily's head snapped up. "Sorry, sir."

"Looks like old Poker Face got out of bed on the wrong side—again," Katy commented. Adjoa and Freema, who sat nearby, giggled.

Lily turned around and grinned at them.

"Okay, class. I'd like you to begin

work on your projects, please. Quietly, if possible!" Mr. Poke ordered.

They were doing the Tudors. Lily was making a collage of Queen Elizabeth I. "I think I'll do her lace ruffle today. I need to get some pieces of paper and stuff from the art cabinet," she said to Katy, who was bent over writing in her notebook.

"Can we have a little more work and a little less talking, Lily Benson?" Mr. Poke drawled.

"Yes, sir," Lily felt herself turning pink as she got up and went to the cabinet. *I wasn't even doing anything,* she thought.

Storm padded over to her. "Are you all right, Lily? You look hot," he woofed.

"I'm fine. Not like *some* people," Lily

murmured, glancing back at the grumpy teacher.

She pulled the cabinet's handle, but it seemed to have gotten stuck. Grasping it more firmly, she pulled again, but the door still wouldn't budge.

"I will help," Storm yapped eagerly.

Lily saw Mr. Poke coming over with a frown on his face. "Uh-oh, you'd better be quick, Storm. Looks like Poker Face is on the war path," she whispered.

Lily felt an odd, warm tingling down her spine as gold sparks ignited in Storm's sandy coat, and the tips of his ears and tail fizzed with power. Something strange was going to happen.

Raising one big sandy front paw, Storm sent a shower of bright golden

sparks whooshing toward the cabinet.
With a faint crackle they sank into the
wood. For a moment nothing happened
and Lily thought Storm's magic hadn't
worked.

"Out of the way, Lily. Let me do it,"
Mr. Poke said irritably, reaching the
cabinet—just as the doors sprang open.

An explosion of papers, brushes, pens,
and paints shot out. Mr. Poke flew
backward as if he'd been blown by a
wind machine and landed on the floor
on his backside.

Rustle! Papers floated down around
him. *Splat!* A plastic jar of glue hit Mr.
Poke on the chest, bursting and
spreading all over his gray sweater.
Thwack! Brushes, pens, and pencils fell
on him, sticking firmly to the glue.

The teacher sat there blinking in shock.

The whole class erupted in laughter. Katy, Adjoa, and Freema were helpless. Lily tried hard to bite back the laughter bubbling up inside her.

"Who packed the cabinet like that?"

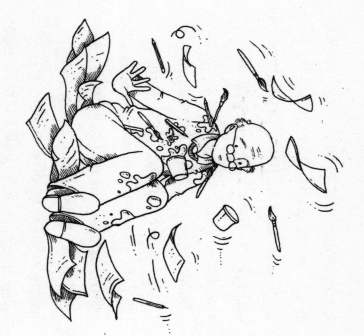

Mr. Poke roared, his face bright red as he scrambled to his feet. "I have to go and get cleaned up. Keep working, class. I'll be right back." He stomped off toward the bathroom, pens and pencils falling with a clatter as he walked away.

"I am sorry, Lily. I think I used too much magic," Storm woofed in dismay.

Making sure that no one was looking, Lily quickly patted him. "You did just fine. It serves Mr. Poke right!"

She began putting everything back into the cabinet. Katy, Freema, and Adjoa helped her. By the time Mr. Poke reappeared wearing a hideous orange, yellow, and brown striped T-shirt, the mess was all cleared up.

The rest of the morning passed quickly, and at lunchtime Lily shared

her cheese sandwiches and chips with
Storm. When they finished, she took
him for a run across the fields. The
excited puppy ran around, chasing
leaves in the wind and tiring himself
out. He spent the rest of the afternoon
napping under Lily's chair.

After school, with Storm back in her
bag, Lily walked home with her
friends.

She paused at the end of her street.
"Did you mean it about me coming
over to see Pixie?" she asked Adjoa.

Adjoa nodded. "Why don't you come
over after school on Friday? We can
both ride Pixie."

"That would be awesome!" Lily said.
She jotted Adjoa's address and phone
number in her notebook before

heading home. "Bye. See you all
tomorrow!" she called.

Katy, Freema, and Adjoa waved as
they walked away.

Just inside her front garden, Lily put
her bag down so that Storm could
jump out. "Adjoa's nice, isn't she?" she
said to him. "I can't wait to meet Pixie."

"Me too!" Storm nodded, his pink
tongue hanging in a doggy grin.

Lily felt a surge of affection for him.

47

She picked Storm up and pet his soft sandy fur. "Having you at school today was awesome! You really taught old Poker Face a lesson. I hope that horrible Shadow never finds you and then you can live with me forever and come to school every day," she said.

"That is not possible, Lily," Storm told her, his small sandy face suddenly serious. "One day I must return to my own world to help heal my mother and fight Shadow."

Lily knew this was true, but she didn't want to believe it. She pushed all thoughts of Storm having to leave out of her mind and thought instead of the fun they would have on Friday with Adjoa and Pixie.

Chapter
★FIVE★

"Here you are, girl." Lily held a piece of carrot on the palm of her hand, so that Pixie could take it with her soft lips. Pixie was a chestnut pony with a white line down her nose and a friendly expression.

Lily turned to Adjoa as the pony crunched the treat. "Pixie is gorgeous!"

Adjoa smiled. "I know. I'm lucky to have her."

Pixie whinnied softly and swiveled her ears.

"I think she agrees with you," Lily said. They both laughed.

Adjoa opened the field gate and Lily helped her saddle the pony and then both girls spent a couple of hours taking turns riding her. Lily thought with a sigh how wonderful it would be to have her own pony and ride her every day.

Storm bounded alongside the pony at first as Lily trotted around the field on her, but his short legs soon got tired. Lily couldn't lift him onto her lap with Adjoa watching. "Are you okay? You're not getting bored?" she leaned down to whisper to him.

"I am fine. I will go and explore," Storm barked softly.

Lily watched him go frolicking off

toward the open-sided, wooden shelter at the bottom of the field. She could see him sniffing all the interesting smells in patches of long grass on the way.

With Storm happily occupied, Lily went back to enjoying her ride. Afterward she helped Adjoa untack Pixie and then rub her down before letting her run free. The pony immediately threw herself onto her back and rolled around. Storm ran straight up to her barking happily.

"Oh no!" Lily gasped, only just stopping herself from calling out to warn Storm to be careful. If Pixie kicked, the tiny puppy could get badly hurt by her hooves.

"What's wrong?" Adjoa asked, frowning.

"Er . . . nothing," Lily murmured, watching tensely as Pixie got to her feet again and shook herself. Her ears flattened as she looked down at the playful puppy, then she leaned down and gently nudged Storm's sandy fur. Storm yapped delightedly, wagging his tail.

Lily gave a big sigh of relief, which she quickly turned into a cough. She turned to Adjoa. "Sorry. I . . . um . . . thought I saw a rat in the straw in Pixie's shelter!"

Adjoa shrugged. "That's no big deal. The farmer's cats will catch it. Let's go in the house and get a drink." She opened the field gate that led straight into her back garden.

"Okay. I'll follow you in a sec. I think I've got a stone in my boot." Bending down so that she had her back to Adjoa, Lily motioned to Storm.

Storm scampered straight over and squeezed under the fence into the back garden. He trotted at Lily's heel, panting happily as they all walked toward the house.

In the kitchen, Adjoa's mom was getting cold drinks from the fridge. "I saw you coming," she said, smiling. "You must be Lily. It's nice to meet you. I'm glad Adjoa's already made a new friend." Her rows of tiny black braids were pinned up into a bun. She wore gold hoop earrings, jeans, and a pretty green top.

"Thanks for the drink, Mrs. Hardiker," Lily said politely.

After their drinks, Lily and Storm went up to Adjoa's room. "It's just like mine!" Lily said delightedly, looking at all the pony posters and books. Red and blue ribbons that Adjoa had won for her riding were pinned around her mirror.

"That was so much fun! Thanks," Lily said to Adjoa before she left for home.

"That's okay. You can come here anytime," Adjoa said, smiling. "See you at school on Monday!"

As she walked away with Storm, Lily was thoughtful. "Adjoa's mom and dad don't seem to have a problem with their daughter taking care of a pony and doing homework. But I don't think I'll *ever* persuade mine to let me have one," she said to him with a sigh.

Storm barked in sympathy, wagging his tail. His thick sandy fur gleamed with tiny golden sparks. "Maybe I can help you," he woofed softly.

The following afternoon, Mrs. Benson dropped Lily and Storm off early at Greengates before she went to her yoga workshop. Lily had been silently thinking about what Storm had said; now she was bursting to ask him about it.

"Did you mean it, about helping me to

get my own pony?" she asked as they walked across the stable yard.

Storm looked at her with alert midnight-blue eyes. "I did, Lily. I always keep my promises."

Lily waited, but Storm didn't say anything more. Her imagination went into overdrive. "I bet you're going to use your magic to make a pony appear out of thin air, aren't you? Are you going to put Mom and Dad into a trance or something, so they let me keep it?" she asked excitedly.

Storm's furry brow dipped in a frown. "No. That would not be the right thing to do, Lily. I am afraid that you will have to be patient," he woofed mysteriously. He leaped forward and went off to explore the yard, shedding a few tiny gold sparks, which glinted in the bright sunlight before dissolving.

Lily stared after Storm. She knew she was going to have to do as he said, but it was hard to be patient when you

wanted something so much.

It was time that she went to see what jobs needed doing, but first Lily went to visit Bandit. She had an apple in her pocket for the pony.

But the palomino wasn't in her stable, so Lily went to check the grazing field. Bandit wasn't there either. As she was walking back across the yard feeling puzzled, Don came out of the tack room holding a saddle.

"Is Bandit out on an early ride?" Lily asked the stable boy.

"No. Bandit's already gone. Didn't Janie tell you?" Don said.

"Gone? Gone where?" Lily asked.

"To her new home," Don explained. "Bandit's quite old now and Janie's been thinking about retiring her for some time. Someone came by during the week and offered Bandit a new home on the spot. Janie jumped at it. Bandit went to live in a field with two goats and a donkey for company."

"Oh, she'll really love that," Lily said, trying hard not to feel sad. But she knew she was really going to miss the gentle old pony.

Don's freckled face crinkled in a smile. "It's amazing that somewhere so perfect came right out of the blue, when Janie hadn't really started looking yet. Just like magic, really. Anyway, see you later." He went off to tack up a pony.

Storm came rushing across the yard, with a dusty nose from where he'd been searching around in some straw.

He gave her a wide doggy grin and flopped down at her feet.

Lily looked down at him thoughtfully. "Did you have anything to do with finding Bandit a perfect new home, by any chance?"

Storm gave her a sideways look. He twitched his nose. "I smell rabbits!" he yelped happily and shot off again toward the grazing field.

Lily stared after him. He was up to something, she was sure of it.

Chapter
★SIX★

It had been another busy afternoon at Greengates. Lily was hanging up a pile of newly cleaned bridles in the tack room.

Janie popped her head in the door. "Why don't you leave that and go have a ride? Tinka's still saddled up."

"Thanks, Janie!" Glancing over to where Storm was napping on top of the brush box, Lily called to him. "Come on, Storm."

Storm's head shot up immediately. He jumped down and padded after Lily to

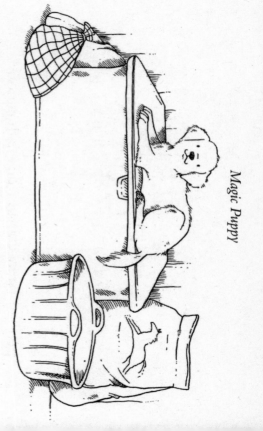

where Tinka was tied to the fence.

Lily buckled on her riding hat before mounting the handsome bay pony. She walked Tinka out of the yard and onto the bridle path. This time she took the fork leading to a field that the riding school had permission to use. Storm ran along beside her, his ears flapping as Lily rode down a tractor path.

Lily had to concentrate very hard when riding Tinka. The bay pony was less experienced than dear old Bandit had been. Lily dismounted and was opening the field gate, when a wood pigeon fluttered up out of a bush. Startled, Tinka threw up her head and danced sideways.

"It's okay, girl." Lily spoke reassuringly, petting Tinka's nose to calm her.

As Tinka backed up, Lily noticed a ditch almost concealed in the long grass by the hedge. Someone had dumped some sharp hawthorn branches in it. Luckily, Tinka had just missed it or she could have been injured. Lily made a mental note to tell Janie about the dangerous ditch when she got back to Greengates.

Storm sat in her lap as Lily continued her ride. But as she made her way back an hour or so later he ran along beside her again. She saw him run off into the field and start jumping around, barking at butterflies and sticking his nose in molehills. By the time Lily got back to the field gate and dismounted again, Storm was behind her.

Lily led Tinka through and was closing the gate, when she spotted a familiar pony and rider coming toward her along the edge of the field. "Look, Storm! It's Adjoa on Pixie!" she cried delightedly.

A moist brown nose and then two sandy ears appeared as Storm squeezed through a small gap in the hedge. He gave an excited bark and leaped toward the long grass.

Lily realized that he was heading straight for the concealed ditch. "Storm!

Look out!" she cried. But the puppy
was so set on reaching his friend Pixie
that he didn't hear her.

Lily threw herself forward. She missed
Storm, but just managed to push him
sideways as she lost her balance and slid
into the ditch.

"Ow!" she gasped with pain as her
ankle twisted and sharp thorns dug into
her leg.

Storm looked down at her in dismay.

"You saved me, Lily. But you are hurt. I will help you," he whined.

"I . . . I think I'm okay," Lily said shakily, biting back tears at the sharp ache in her leg. Her riding pants were torn and smeared with grass stains.

Time seemed to stand still. Lily felt a familiar warm tingling down her back as vivid gold sparks ignited in Storm's fur. His tail stiffened and crackled with power. Raising a velvety front paw Storm sent a whoosh of sparks fizzing toward Lily's injured leg. For a second the pain increased and then it drained away just as if someone had poured it down a drain.

When the bright sparks faded, Lily saw that her riding pants were

A New Beginning

clean and fixed, too. "Thanks, Storm," she whispered.

"You are welcome," Storm woofed as the final gold sparks faded from his thick sandy fur.

Lily quickly climbed out of the ditch. She stood up as Adjoa pulled Pixie to a halt a couple of feet away. "Watch out for this ditch. You can hardly see it. I . . . er . . . nearly just slipped right into . . ." she blustered. Lily racked her brain for an explanation that didn't involve Storm, but Adjoa wasn't listening.

Her new friend's eyes were red and puffy. It was obvious that Adjoa had been crying. Lily felt sad for her friend. What could be wrong?

Lily held Tinka by her reins and listened with growing dismay to what Adjoa had to say.

"The farmer who we rent Pixie's field from is selling it and we can't find another field nearby. Mom and Dad say it would cost too much to put her into stables where she'd be cared for, and so we might have to sell her," Adjoa said tearfully.

"Oh no! That's terrible," Lily exclaimed, putting one arm around her friend.

She knew it was expensive to have a

pony looked after by a stable. But it was awful to think of Adjoa losing her beloved pony.

Beside her Pixie gave a friendly blow and dipped her head to nuzzle Storm gently. The tiny puppy was lying on his back in the grass with all four legs in the air, showing his fat pale tummy. For once, Lily felt too upset for Adjoa to smile at his playful antics.

An idea came to her. She was going to talk to her parents.

Chapter
SEVEN

"I'm sorry, Lily. But my answer has to be the same," Mrs. Benson said.

They were all sitting in the kitchen on Saturday evening. Storm was lying down next to Lily's chair, invisible to everyone except her, as usual. Lily had just finished explaining about Pixie in the hope that her parents might be willing to buy the pony.

"I agree with your mom," Mr. Benson said. "Looking after a pony is a big responsibility. We're just not sure this is the right time for you to take that on."

"But it is, Dad! I'd be the best pony owner ever!" Lily said in her best pleading voice. "And if we bought Pixie, Adjoa could still see her whenever she wanted."

Her dad smiled and reached out to ruffle her hair. "I'm sorry, honey. I feel bad for Adjoa, too, but the subject's closed."

"That's what I thought you'd say," Lily said, sighing heavily.

All that evening and throughout Sunday, Adjoa and Pixie were on Lily's mind. On Monday, when she and Storm walked to school, they met up with Katy and Freema, but Adjoa wasn't with them.

"Where's Adjoa?" Lily asked.

"She's not coming in today. My aunt says she's got an upset tummy," Freema explained.

"I know *why* Adjoa's tummy is upset. It's because she's so worried about what's going to happen to Pixie," Lily said sadly.

Freema and Katy nodded.

When they reached the coatroom, Lily hung back and let her friends go into school ahead of her. "I wish I could think of a way to help Adjoa keep Pixie," she whispered to Storm. "But I've already tried Mom and Dad. I don't know what else I can do."

Storm whined softly in sympathy and then his big midnight-blue eyes lit up. "You could talk to the lady who runs the riding stables," he suggested.

"Janie? I can't see what good that would do," Lily said, frowning.

Storm barked encouragingly, wagging his tail and dancing around her feet in circles. Lily smiled. "Well, okay then, if you're that sure it'll help. We'll stop over there tonight after school. Uh-oh! Watch out! Mr. Poke just came in. We'd better go into class!" she hissed out of the side of her mouth.

Back home after school, Lily quickly changed into her jeans and T-shirt, before running downstairs. She found her mom in the kitchen. "Could you give me a ride over to Greengates, please?" she asked.

Her mom looked surprised. "Don't you get enough of that place on the weekends? Why do you want to go over there now?"

Lily thought quickly. "Tinka was sick on Saturday. I wanted to check and see if she's any better," she lied.

Mrs. Benson smiled. "That's nice of you. You're a sweet person, Lily Benson."

Lily blushed, feeling a little guilty. But there was no way she could tell her mom that it was Storm's suggestion to go and talk to Janie. Anyway, it was true that she was always happy to see Tinka and all the other ponies. "So can I have a ride?" she asked.

Her mom nodded. "We'll go now. I have to go to the supermarket, so I can drop you off at Greengates and then pick you up on my way back."

Lily sat in the back of the car, with Storm on her lap as they drove there. She got out of the car at Greengates's main entrance. "Thanks for the ride, Mom. I'll see you later."

As soon as her mom had driven away, Lily went into the yard. Storm trotted purposefully at her heels, invisible as usual.

She could see Janie sitting at her computer through the office window.

Lily paused, feeling uncertain. "Well, here I am. But I'm still not sure why! What am I supposed to say to her?" she whispered to Storm.

The puppy's luminous midnight-blue eyes looked even brighter than usual. "I think you should tell Janie about how Pixie needs a home," he woofed.

Lily frowned. "But there's no point. Greengates isn't a stable. It's a riding school. And anyway, Janie doesn't have

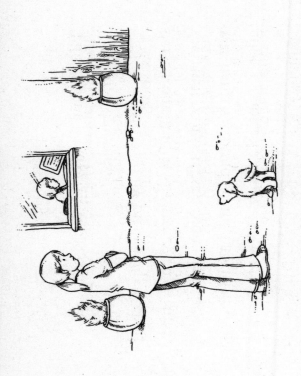

room for any extra ponies. All the loose boxes are full."

Storm pricked his ears. "Not all of them."

Lily blinked as she realized what Storm was hinting at. "You're right! Bandit's not here anymore."

Storm nodded, looking very pleased with himself.

Before Lily could ask him anything else, Janie came out into the yard. "Lily?

This is a nice surprise. What can I do for you?" she said.

"I . . . um . . ." Lily bit her lip, feeling herself blushing as she struggled to find the right words to say. Now that she was here, her mind seemed to have gone completely blank.

Chapter
★EIGHT★

Storm gave a gentle woof and as Lily
looked down into his sparkling
midnight-blue eyes, she felt herself
starting to calm down.

Lily took a deep breath and suddenly
it all came pouring out. "I . . . um . . .
wanted to ask you something. I've got a
friend named Adjoa who's got a pony
named Pixie. She's very sweet-natured,
but the farmer who owns her field is
selling it. And I thought, well, I was
hoping—"

Janie smiled. "Whoa! Slow down a

bit. Let's go into my office, Lily. I could use a break from working on my accounts. We'll have a cold drink and you can tell me all about it."

A few minutes later, Lily sat sipping her apple juice as Janie tapped her fingers on the desk thoughtfully.

"So what you're really asking is for me to put Pixie into the stable?" she said to Lily.

Lily nodded, feeling encouraged by Janie's calmness and willingness to listen. Everything seemed to have slotted into place and become clear in her mind. Now Lily knew exactly what to say.

"What about if Pixie lives here *and* works as one of the riding school ponies? Adjoa would have to agree, but I think she'd do anything if it meant

she could keep Pixie. She'd still own her, so she'd help look after her and pay for Pixie's food and bedding and stuff. But it probably wouldn't cost anywhere near as much as a normal stable."

"You seem to have this all worked out," Janie said.

"I do!" Lily said firmly.

"Hmm. It could work. We've had arrangements like this in the past and we are a pony short now that Bandit's gone. But I'd have to try Pixie out before I decided that she was right for Greengates. She'd have to be gentle, friendly, and dependable."

"Oh, she is! She's perfect. Should I ask Adjoa's parents to call you and set up a meeting?" Lily asked eagerly.

Janie nodded, smiling. "Yes. You're one determined young lady, Lily Benson."

"That's what my dad says!" Lily beamed at Janie as she got up. "Thanks so much, Janie. Is it okay if I go and see Tinka and the other ponies? I have just enough time before Mom picks me up."

"Of course it is. I'll leave you to it. I'd better get back to these accounts."

Lily and Storm spent twenty minutes

with the ponies before going back to the riding stable's entrance. Mrs. Benson had just arrived and was waiting to pick her up.

On the way home in the back of the car, Lily stroked Storm's floppy sandy ears. "You had this all worked out, didn't you," she said softly.

Storm nodded. "But I could not have

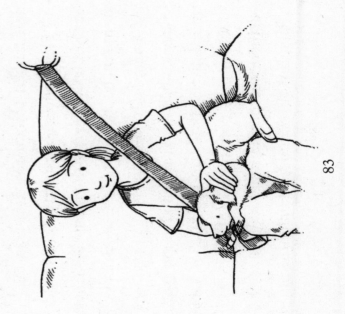

done it all by myself. It was you who spoke to Janie. You did it, Lily."

Lily felt a warm glow of pride. It felt good to have helped her friend. "I can't wait to tell Adjoa all about it. I'm going to call her as soon as I get home."

The moment her mom pulled into the driveway, Lily shot out of the car and dashed toward the house.

"Er, excuse me, young lady! I could use some help with the groceries," her mom called after her.

"Sorry," Lily said sheepishly.

She rushed back, grabbed some bags, and dumped them on the kitchen table.

As she was coming out of the kitchen, the phone rang.

It was Adjoa's mom. "Hello, Lily. Is

Adjoa with you? Can I have a word
with her, please?" she asked.

"She isn't here," Lily replied, puzzled.

"Oh my, I was hoping she'd ridden
Pixie over to see you," Mrs. Hardiker
said, sounding worried. "Could I talk to
your mom?"

Lily passed the phone over. "It's
Adjoa's mom."

Lily waited impatiently while the two

moms spoke. "What's going on?" she asked as her mom hung up the phone.

"Adjoa left a note saying she couldn't handle giving up Pixie, and some of her clothes are missing. Mrs. Hardiker was hoping she'd come over here. But it's beginning to look like Adjoa has run away with Pixie."

"Oh no!" Lily gasped.

Chapter
NINE

"It'll be dark soon. Adjoa must be so scared. We have to find her and tell her the news about Greengates!" Lily said to Storm as soon as they were alone in her bedroom.

Storm nodded. "I will take us to Adjoa's house and see if I can pick up a fresh trail."

Lily felt a familiar warm tingling down her back as gold sparks crackled in Storm's sandy fur and a fountain of golden glitter streamed out of his tail. There was a bright flash and a whooshing sensation and suddenly Lily found herself standing with Storm outside Pixie's field at the back of Adjoa's house.

Storm sniffed around, picking up Pixie's scent. Moments later, he stiffened. Lily saw that his moist brown nose was glowing like a gold nugget. "This way!" he barked, setting off at a run.

Lily followed Storm away from the field and through the streets. They hurried along the main road and then toward the edge of town. The street lights had already come on. Overhead the first stars had begun twinkling in the sky.

Lily grew hot and sweaty as she and Storm followed Pixie's trail, but she wasn't tired. Gold sparks flashed past her as Storm's magic made them travel in double-quick time. Gradually Lily realized where they were heading.

"Greengates is just over there. Adjoa must have taken the bridle path. I bet she's planning to hide in the woods overnight. She'll probably take the short cut across the fields," she told Storm.

A few minutes later, Storm barked and wagged his tail. "Over there!"

In the twilight, Lily could just make out the figure of a pony and rider against the shadowy bushes. The moon came out from behind a cloud and Lily could see more clearly. "It's them!" she cried.

Lily saw that Pixie was trotting toward the familiar field gate. "That ditch! Adjoa's heading straight for it. Those prickly branches have been cleared away since I told Janie about it, but a pony could still break her leg if she stumbles into it. I bet she's too upset to remember it's there and Pixie won't see it in the dark!"

Storm's midnight-blue eyes flashed. Another rainbow of sparks shot out ahead of him and he leaped forward into the stream of light. Lily felt herself shooting through the air beside him. She and Storm landed a few feet in front of Adjoa and Pixie.

Lily walked forward, holding up her arms. "It's me, Lily! Adjoa, stop!"

Adjoa reined Pixie in. The pony's ears swiveled and her head came up, but she halted calmly a few paces away from the ditch.

"Lily! What are you doing here? How did you find me?" Adjoa cried.

"Don't worry about that now," Lily said. "That ditch I fell into the other day is right in front of you. Pixie could have stumbled into it. Come over here. I have to tell you something."

Adjoa urged Pixie over to one side,

but she didn't dismount. She looked shaken, but determined. "Thanks for reminding me about that ditch. But if you're going to try and persuade me to go back home, don't bother!" Adjoa said, looking down at Lily.

"Adjoa, listen! I've got some great news," Lily said quickly before her friend could decide to ride away. "I talked with Janie at Greengates. She's willing to take Pixie into her stable on the condition that you let her be used for the riding school."

"Really?" Adjoa looked stunned, but her hands loosened on the reins. Her shoulders relaxed as she thought about it. "I wouldn't mind little kids riding Pixie and she'd enjoy the extra exercise. Dad said she was getting a bit fat

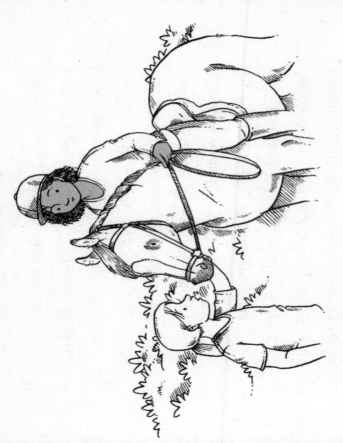

anyway. But even with Janie using Pixie for rides, it's still going to cost a lot to keep her stabled at Greengates. I still don't know if Mom and Dad will agree."

Lily's face fell. She hadn't thought of this. It seemed as if there was a flaw in her awesome plan.

Storm jumped up with his paws on

Lily's leg and woofed for attention. Lily looked down at him. "You could ask your mom and dad to help," he suggested in a soft bark.

It was a few seconds before Storm's words sank in. "That's it!" she burst out, her eyes widening.

"What is?" Adjoa said, puzzled.

"I just had a brilliant idea. Come on, Adjoa. We're going back to talk to my parents!" She quickly outlined her plan.

A look of hope came over Adjoa's face. "Do you think they'll agree?"

"They have to. It's Pixie's last chance," Lily said determinedly, turning on her heel, confident that Adjoa would now follow her on Pixie. At her side, Storm gave an encouraging yelp.

Chapter
★TEN★

Later that evening, Lily sat at the kitchen table eating a pizza with her mom and dad. Storm was curled up under the table.

"You did a great job persuading Adjoa to come home," her dad said. "Her parents were almost out of their minds with worry. They've been on the phone saying how great you are. Good work, sweetie."

Lily felt herself blushing. "Anyone would have done the same."

"I'm not sure that's true," her mom

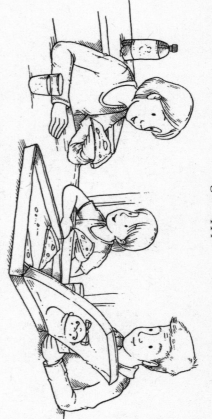

said, patting her hand. "What I still can't figure out is how you found her so quickly and got up to the field near Greengates in record time."

"It must be all the exercise I've been doing. Mmm. This pizza's delish!" Lily said, quickly changing the subject. She slipped a small piece under the table for Storm to munch. "Mo-om? Da-ad?" she said in a persuading voice. "I've . . . um . . . got something to ask you."

Her parents exchanged glances. "I hope this isn't about having your own pony again!" Mrs. Benson said.

"Of course it's not," Lily said brightly.

"Thank goodness for that!" her dad said.

Lily paused for effect. "It's about me having half a pony!"

Mr. Benson frowned. "Run that by me again."

Lily grinned. "What I really mean is *sharing* a pony!" She explained about Janie agreeing to take Pixie into the stable and being a riding school pony.

"But it's still going to be very expensive, so Adjoa's parents might decide to sell Pixie anyway. But they won't if we help with the costs. And then I'd be sort of sharing a pony with

Adjoa. I'd be able to groom Pixie and ride her sometimes. What do you think?"

"I think Pixie's going to be one busy pony!" her dad said, smiling. "But it's an interesting idea."

Lily held her breath and had all her fingers and toes crossed. At least her dad hadn't said no right away like he usually did.

"I know you, Lily. You'll want to be up at Greengates every night, looking after Pixie and grooming her," said Mrs. Benson. "I'm still worried that your schoolwork could suffer."

"I know I might want to do that, but I won't, because I'll know that I have to take turns with Adjoa," Lily said honestly. "I'll just be so happy to be able to ride Pixie sometimes—and pretend she's all mine until I get a pony of my own one day!"

Her mom and dad exchanged glances.

"Well, when you put it like that, it sounds like a fair arrangement," her mom said.

"And it's the only way Lily's ever going to give us any peace! So the answer's yes," her dad added.

"Yay!" Lily flung herself at her parents and gave them both huge hugs and then did a little dance around the table. "I can't wait to tell Adjoa!"

Storm ran out from under the table and jumped up and down, barking excitedly. Lily grinned and just barely managed to stop herself from bending down and picking him up.

Later that night, Lily closed her bedroom curtains, getting ready for bed.

Outside in the street she saw a couple of people taking their dogs for a walk. She jumped into bed and snuggled up under the blankets with Storm.

"Thanks so much for everything, Storm. You kept your promise about helping me get a pony, even though things turned out differently than how I imagined! You're the most awesome friend ever. We're going to have an amazing summer with Pixie and Adjoa!"

Storm tucked his head under her chin. "I am glad I was able to help."

Suddenly Lily heard howling and growling from outside in the street. She jumped back out of bed and peered through the bedroom curtains. The two dog walkers were struggling to control their dogs, which were pulling at their leashes and looking up at her bedroom. In the light of the street lamps, the dogs' eyes looked pale and were glowing.

"That's weird . . ." Lily said, turning to Storm.

The tiny puppy was hiding in the bed. She could see him trembling with fright.

Frowning, Lily glanced outside again and saw the dogs suddenly calm down. After a moment, their confused owners walked on until they were out of sight.

Lily came back to Storm. As she went to pet him she realized that he was still shaking all over. "What's wrong? Are you sick?" she asked worriedly.

Storm shook his head. His ears were laid back and his tail was tucked beneath him. "I sense that Shadow is close. I think he used his magic, so that the dogs outside would attack me."

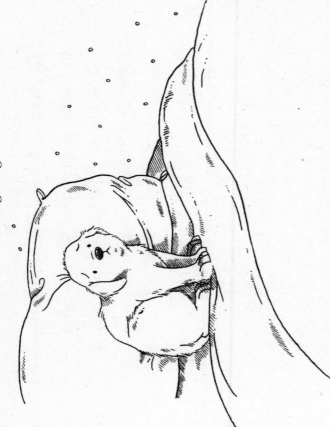

Lily looked at her friend in dismay.

"Is that what he'll do if he finds you?"

Storm nodded, his eyes as dull as blue stones. "All the dogs around here will be looking for me now. I will use my magic to mask my scent. It may give me a little more time."

Lily kissed the top of his sandy head,

breathing in his sweet puppy smell, and lay awake, hoping that Storm would be safe. She didn't think she could bear it if she never saw him again.

Chapter

★ ELEVEN ★

Lily woke up with a start the next morning. To her relief, Storm was curled up asleep next to her.

He seemed more like his normal self, but his sparkling midnight-blue eyes were still concerned. "I will stay here and hide. I want to be sure that Shadow cannot sense where I am," he barked.

Lily felt reluctant to leave him, but she had promised to meet Adjoa at Greengates and help settle Pixie into her new home.

"I'll see you later," she said, bending

down to kiss the top of Storm's warm silky head.

Storm curled himself into a tight ball and didn't answer.

"Whoa, there, girl!" Janie Green said gently.

Lily and Adjoa stood watching as Janie backed Pixie out of the horse trailer, hitched to her Land Rover.

"That's it. Good. Come on."

Pixie slowly moved backward, step by step. Finally she stood in the stable yard, her legs trembling slightly and her chestnut coat twitching.

"Good girl," Adjoa said gently, going over to pet Pixie's nose. "She's feeling nervous. She's been used to living in a field by herself."

"It's only natural for her to feel unsettled," Janie said understandingly. "She's used to you, so why don't you and Lily lead her around for a little before you take her into the loose box? Call me if you have any problems. Okay?"

"Okay. Thanks." Adjoa looked over at Lily as Janie went to park her Land Rover. "Janie's really nice, isn't she?"

Lily smiled and nodded. "There are lots of strange new smells here. Why don't you walk Pixie past the grazing field a few times? It might calm her if she smells fresh grass like in her field," she suggested to Adjoa.

"That's a good idea."

For the next twenty minutes Adjoa led Pixie around the yard, talking gently to her the entire time.

Lily watched, trying not to think about Storm and whether he was still safe. But her worries about her tiny puppy friend kept pushing into her mind.

Pixie gradually seemed to relax.

Finally, Adjoa felt confident enough to lead her to Bandit's old loose box, which was going to be her new home. Earlier, Lily had covered it with a deep layer of clean bedding. There was a hay net hanging up and clean water in a bucket.

Lily opened the door wide.

Adjoa went to lead Pixie inside. But Pixie rolled her eyes and stood still.

"Come on. It's lovely in there. There's space for you to turn around and lie down if you want to," she encouraged.

Pixie shifted nervously and rolled her eyes. "She's just not comfortable with going indoors," Adjoa said.

"I'll get some carrots from the feed store. That might tempt her to go in," Lily said.

"Good idea," Adjoa said gratefully. Lily returned quickly. But the carrots didn't work either.

"What if we can't get Pixie to go in at all?" Adjoa said worriedly. "Janie might change her mind about her. She won't want an awkward pony at the riding school."

"That's not going to happen. Pixie's just scared. She's going to be fine," Lily said reassuringly, but she was starting to get concerned.

If only Storm was here. He'd calm Pixie down. But Storm had to fight his own battle, hiding from his enemy—the fierce wolf Shadow.

"I think I'd better go and get Janie or Don, after all," Lily decided reluctantly after another fifteen minutes of leading

Pixie around and a second failed attempt at getting her to go into her box.

"Okay, then." Adjoa was almost in tears.

Just then Lily heard a rustling sound from inside the loose box. A spurt of bright golden sparks shot up out of the straw and a cute sandy face appeared.

"Storm!" Lily exclaimed delightedly and then realized that Adjoa was giving her a strange look. "I mean . . . it looks like rain or something. I think we should try Pixie one more time before we go and get help."

Adjoa looked doubtful, but she nodded.

Pixie stretched out her neck and blew a warm breath toward Storm. Storm barked encouragingly and wagged his tail.

Pixie lifted one front leg. She took a step forward and then another one. She went inside and Adjoa closed the door after her. "Phew! At last! I thought she'd never go in," she said, relieved.

"She'll be fine now. Why don't you go and tell Janie?" Lily suggested.

Just as Adjoa disappeared into the office, Storm whined in terror. He leaped over the stable door into the yard, trailing

a bright comet's tail of golden sparks and streaked toward the tack room.

Lily whipped around and saw two small dogs coming through the main gates. They raised their heads and she saw their abnormally long teeth and fierce pale wolf eyes. Her heart skipped a beat. They were here for Storm!

She dashed across the yard and rushed into the empty tack room.

There was a bright golden flash.

Lily blinked hard as her vision cleared. Storm stood there as his magnificent real self. The majestic young wolf's dazzling silver-gray fur gleamed and his midnight-blue eyes glowed like sapphires. A she-wolf with a gentle tired face stood next to Storm.

And then Lily knew that this time Storm was leaving for good.

"Our enemies are very close. We must go!" Storm's mother rumbled.

Storm raised a large silver paw in farewell. "You have been a good friend. Be of good heart, Lily," he said in a deep velvety growl.

Lily's throat closed with tears and there was an ache in her chest. She was going to miss Storm terribly. "Good-bye, Storm. Take care. I'll never forget you," she whispered hoarsely.

There was a final bright flash and a crackle of gold sparks that sprinkled down around her like warm rain.

Storm and his mother faded and then disappeared. The dogs ran into the tack room. Lily saw their teeth and eyes instantly return to normal before they turned and slunk away.

Lily blinked away tears as she went slowly back out into the yard. At least she'd had a chance to say good-bye to Storm. She knew she'd never forget the wonderful adventure she'd shared with the magic puppy.

Although she could never tell another person about Storm, there was someone else who was going to miss the tiny puppy and with whom she could share all her thoughts. Pixie!

As Lily went toward Pixie's stall and saw Adjoa coming out of Janie's office, she smiled at the thought of all the adventures they were going to have with their very own pony!

About the Author

Sue Bentley's books for children often include animals, fairies, and wildlife. She lives in Northampton and enjoys reading, going to the movies, relaxing by her garden pond, and watching the birds feeding their babies on the lawn. At school she was always getting yelled at for daydreaming or staring out of the window—but she now realizes that she was storing up ideas for when she became a writer. She has met and owned many cats and dogs, and each one has brought a special kind of magic to her life.

Magic Puppy